12 TWELVE WOW SHORT STORIES

You'll find heavy doses of nail-biting exploits, a profusion of surprise endings and a mixed bag of loveable characters ... in addition to chills up the spine, flippant forays and two real-life adventures for your reading pleasure.

by Frank Tumbeity
and his charming wife
Lynn

Printed and bound in the United States of America
First printing • ISBN 978-0-9998884-7-6
Copyright © 2018

FOR ORDER INFORMATION VISIT
www.scottpublishingcompany.com/store

 **SCOTT COMPANY PUBLISHING**
P.O. Box 9707 • Kalispell, MT 59904
Toll Free: 1-800-628-0212
Fax: 1-406-756-0098

This medley of short stories is dedicated to two special voracious readers, our children.

Table of Contents

Story 1

Alert! Alert!

Stay vigilant, buckle up and prepare for an adventure the likes of which you can't imagine. Now ... turn the page and let the games begin!

Games

"Someone's in the house," she whispers through the darkness. "I can feel it in my bones. Please, please take a look downstairs, Mock! Our three boys are there!"

Rooted to the top step, she gazes into the emptiness of night. The sound of her husband's ratty old slippers shuffling along the hallway ceases. "MOCK, WHERE ARE YOU?" she cries, then descends the steps and heads for the boys' bedroom. She finds their door ajar and peers inside. An orange glow dances along the far wall. Shadowy forms loom over empty beds. The woman staggers backward at the sight. A powerful arm slips around her waist. Something cold clamps over her mouth. Her last muffled words, "What have you done with my children?" go unanswered.

The disappearance of the family grabbed widespread attention after it was learned another, with two teenage girls, had previously vanished from the same isolated region of Montana – a boiler room of gossip for decades. Some believe the teenagers were the intended targets and their parents mere afterthoughts. As the story unfolded, there was considerable speculation regarding the authorities' apparent refusal to take those abductions all that seriously. Time moves on, but the incidents weren't forgotten.

Accessible by one dirt road tucked between snowcapped Mission Mountains, the remote alleged crime scene looks harmless to the casual observer brave enough to explore the area. Fed by a crystal clear stream, towering Douglas firs and assorted pines, most traces of previous human habitation have been washed away or grown over in this isolated region of despair. Even two building foundations were first reduced to rubble before being consumed by Mother Nature's progressions. This scenic expanse was rarely visited in the past one hundred plus years, its ominous reputation the reason. There are those that suggest aggressive Bigfoot populations were the culprits and roam the back country to this day while others attribute extraterrestrials to the disappearances. More rational folks believe the hapless families simply moved on due to the lack of job opportunities. Some believe this entire affair was nothing more than a fictitious story. If not fictitious, how did the writers learn so much about the abductions, especially the mother's plea for her children?

An adventurous pimply faced young fellow who goes by the name of Slap Shot always wanted to enter this pristine realm of uncertainty. One evening a mysterious cloaked figure leaves a black box on the front porch then melts into the night. First thinking it's a joke, Slap Shot doesn't tell his parents. On the other hand, the parcel might be for his amusement. Several pairs of goggles and a small electronic gadget are inside. Simply punch in your desired destination according to the instructions, slip on the goggles, flip the switch and you're off. Finally, not having any of it, he selects the backyard swimming pool as the target – his second mistake. His first was not reading all the instructions and not taking this seriously. Goggles in place, switch flipped and finding the affair amusing, he unwittingly plunges into the deep end of the pool. The poor fellow can't swim. Drenched and going under, swirling water separates him from his headset. Goggles fall to the bed, and he returns mentally to his room dry as a desert toad.

"WHOOPEE! It seemed so real, unbelievably lifelike. I've got to be more careful next time where I go. This game is better than any I ever played, but I don't have a feel for its shortcomings. I'm sure it is a game or something like one."

His next objective will be nothing less than a dream come true, investigating the mystery surrounding those family disappearances. Everyone living around the lower Missions still talks about the strange tragedies. They do it in hushed tones of course. The way people treat the events always intrigued him.

Preparation for the trek begins in his bedroom, tens of miles from his intended destination. Many stories about the abductions, even interesting scuttlebutt, exist in numerous articles written about the so called ill-fated families. Wanting to refresh his memory, he can't be more excited as he digests several favorite magazine articles he had saved.

When finished reading, the young man shouts down the steps, "I'm off Mom. Wish me the best." There is no response. She apparently doesn't hear.

Slap Shot can't leave his cat home. Kitty, a nice size cougar, actually little more than an overgrown pussycat, loves him to pieces. The feline follows her human buddy everywhere, so naturally he fits her with a small pair of goggles. Slap Shot couldn't have a better companion. She communicates using body language and several defining noises only the young man can interpret. A cougar smells, hears and sees things Slap Shot only wishes he could.

Goggles in place, he once again flips the switch and begins his trek through the darkness on the only dirt road into the backcountry. Slap Shot hadn't anticipated traveling at night. Mock, his wife and three boys disappeared in the emptiness of night. The idea makes him a bit jittery. A chill shoots up his spine. Gradually, as time wears on his outlook changes. He's watching Kitty enjoy her outing: trying to catch her tail, rubbing against trees. By her actions, no one knows they are there. He decides to leave surveillance up to his humungous pussycat.

Slap Shot didn't bring a flashlight, only a walking stick. Hopefully, a full moon will show him the way. Moonlight shining amongst trees creates shadows of many shapes. A few resemble men, others the formidable Grizzly. His heart begins to race again. No reactions from Kitty means … well, all is OK. He calms down some.

An opening in the woods to the right reveals a stream rippling over rounded rocks, centuries old. The swift running water sparkles in the light of the moon. Up ahead a road not much bigger than a path shoots left straight as an arrow off the main road.

"Well, Kitty, which way do we go?"

She puts her nose to the ground and sniffs several times then repeats the process. Nothing arouses her curiosity. Shortly, her head raises, nostrils flare. Her eyes point down the smaller dirt road. Her rigid stance informs Slap Shot something living is ahead. She is a predatory creature after all, so it's not appetizing or Kitty would be more excited.

"Let's see what it is girl."

Kitty leads the way guided by her nose. Slap Shot follows cautiously. Keeping off the road, the adventurers proceed through knee high weeds parallel to the little road. From time to time Kitty stops, raises her nose, sniffs then slinks onward. Whatever she scents is on the move too far ahead to see at night. Trees to his right tend to block the moonlight. Finally, Kitty stops and hunkers down. Slap Shot assumes she is nearing her quarry. He sees nothing in the impenetrable darkness. Nevertheless he, too, crouches down. Soon the cougar moves forward, still keeping low in the weeds. An abrupt turn right brings the pair into a field. Kitty's muscles tense as she slowly advances … then stops. Slap Shot still sees nothing. Finally, he spots a house cat facing his cougar. Kitty lowers her head in a friendly gesture to touch the little puss cat's nose with hers.

"I'll be darn. Doesn't that beat all," he says.

Little puss cat raises a paw and lets out a mighty hiss making Slap Shot jump backwards. Kitty, too, reacts by taking one mighty leap into his arms. Eighty pounds of cat hit Slap Shot squarely in the chest sending him flying. He lands on his back with a cougar staring him in the face. Feeling remorseful Kitty proceeds to lick Slap Shot's face with her sandpaper tongue.

"Yuck, Kitty, I've asked you never to do that … come on!"

By the time the two reclaim their dignity, the little victorious puss cat is gone.

While Slap Shot regains his feet, he notices Kitty standing straight as a teacher's pointer shaft, not moving a muscle. "What's up girl?" She remains determined.

She's facing enormous silhouettes. Towering Douglas firs bracket what appears to be the shape of a structure well below the forest treetops.

"I can't believe what we're seeing, Kitty." Moving closer a chimney materializes on the skyline. "I'll be darned, it's a house alright. This doesn't exist according to my info." But it does, and moving closer an opened window becomes visible from a dull fireplace glow. Looking inside the smallish home, several wooden chairs and a bench surround the hearth.

Suddenly a distraught woman shatters the silence. "MOCK, WHERE ARE YOU!" Seconds pass and she appears shuffling toward a slightly opened door. Someone grabs her and quickly pulls her into the other room, the one with an orange glow. Slap Shot hears her respond in a muffled voice. "What have you done with my children?"

Kitty doesn't like the woman being jostled. "YOWL!" she howls.

"Oh, darn!" Concern distorts Slap Shot's young face, and they run for the woods as the visible moon blinks on between puffy clouds.

Too late, the two intruders spot them and rush to the opened window, revolvers drawn. POW, POW.

"Whoa, that second shot was close. It hit my walking stick." The two keep running when they hear the front door bang open.

Slap Shot stops to catch his breath after he decides they aren't pursued. Time passes. The two move on. Scampering helter-skelter until dawn, they become lost in a sea of trees.

"There's an opening in the woods, Kitty. Let's see if I can figure out our location." A house looms up ahead. "Oh great, we've been running in circles all this time. The abductions took place right over there."

Not knowing where the abductors are Slap Shot decides to keep to the forest and watch the house. A team of horses and a wagon are parked out front. Furniture, beds and packed boxes have been loaded into the back. Two adults and three young people rush out the front door carrying personal items, Mock with a rifle, and leap onto the wagon. The horses are urged to walk on. Wooden wheels rattle down the long driveway and onto the dirt road.

"Well, they escaped, Kitty, thanks to us leading the bad guys on a merry trip through the woods. Speaking of bad guys, I wonder what happened to them?"

"We're right behind you, you spoilers."

Turning, Slap Shot stares at a revolver pointing between his eyes … inches away. A second man has Kitty in his sights. The young adventurer reaches down with one hand and grips Kitty's goggle strap, at the same time grabbing his.

"It's nothing personal … goodbye!" the first man says and begins to squeeze the revolver trigger.

POW! POW! Two deadly shots are fired … into empty space.

Slap Shot and Kitty find themselves standing in the room where the quest first began, Mom calling them to supper.

"What a game this is. Our adventure seemed so real to me, and the kidnappers were nothing more than two bad guys, not extraterrestrials or a Bigfoot bunch. Think we changed history today, Kitty?"

Both are hungry. The famished duo steals down the steps. Two pair of goggles remained on the bed beside one walking stick, the one with a chunk taken out of it by a bullet intended for Slap Shot.

Story 2

INTRO

Have you ever in your life heard of a peanut butter sandwich caper – probably not. Well, let this be the first. Turn to the next page and begin a different kind of whodunit.

The Peanut Butter Sandwich Caper

No matter how trivial the goods, I don't find pilfering acceptable. Don't laugh, but in this case the villain took a peanut butter sandwich. I had parked and locked my mountain bike in a two-wheeler rack alongside a jogging trail next to a park. The trail was on the edge of town, not more than a 10 minute pedal from home. Since several picnic tables were close by, I brought my meager but tasty supper with me after work: two sammies, an apple and a candy bar.

The trail, according to what I had read, is a three mile oval, starting and ending by a boulder the size of a compact car. I couldn't wait to get started as I focused my attention on a smooth, inviting dirt trail, so off I jogged. It was nice running under shade trees. Upon returning and dripping sweat, I plopped down exhausted on a park bench close to my bike. Immediately, I noticed the paper bag containing my mouthwatering supper looked open behind the bike seat. Damn, one of my peanut butter sammies was gone.

Someone must have spied my bag of goodies in the little wire basket and helped themselves. Scanning the area for suspects seemed to be easily done. Hardly anyone was around. I'm not normally observant, don't pay attention to most everyday activities and above all don't rightly care. For months I thought Wikileaks was a bladder malfunction, so you see, I won't make much of a detective. Besides, all this flatfoot stuff is new to me. It is beginning to arouse my curiosity though. Detective matters do kinda sound fun.

Now for looking into whodunit: Situated not more than 50 feet away, I couldn't help noticing a grandmother type draped over a park bench reading a book while her young charge, just then, jumped off monkey bars and headed for a close by swing set. Neither one seemed to be suspicious to me at first glance. Wait a sec, I said to myself, the woman had a piece of crumpled up wax paper beside her – ha, ha. Well … maybe she is a suspect after all. The balled up paper was the same kind of wrapping used for my sammies. Hmmm, this is becoming a most interesting caper. Move over Sherlock, make room for me.

Now for checking out the only other person in the park, that would be the grounds keeper. At this time, he happened to be at the far end loading several trash buckets into his truck. As I recall, before my jog the man was wiping tables likely dirtied by the lunch crowd. Since my bike is parked next to a picnic bench, it's safe to assume he had passed right by it. Meaning, the man had access to my lunch, a brilliant deduction on my part.

No reason to hang around here anymore; so, I decided to take off for home and chalk up today's outing as a learning experience. Discovering the snitch's identity seemed improbable since the evidence was likely eaten. Considering the facts, this case is unsolvable, therefore should be forgotten on this fine Monday evening.

Actually, in thinking about work related problems I did forget. When time came for my next jog on Wednesday evening, I brought my lunch with me like before. Everything went down the same … even one of my peanut butter sammies was pilfered – damn. No, make that a double DAMN!

Immediately, I spotted the book worm munching on a peanut butter sammy as she read. I never ran harder in my life. I wanted to nail that crafty sneak red-handed. She had already eaten half her heist when I pulled up directly in front of her. I was as mad as an agitated hornet.

Grandma put her book down before greeting me. "What in the hell do you want, SONNY?"

"Why did you steal my peanut butter sandwich, MADAM?" The little Belgian couldn't have said it much better.

She beckoned for me to come closer. Then … she pulled open the sammy and sliced pieces of hotdog fell out as she proceeded to introduce me to both bread halves by smearing the contents on my face. Actually, the mustard I'd mistaken for peanut butter tasted pretty good. Maybe I should have asked her for the brand. Well anyway, upon returning to my bike humiliated, I spotted a raven not more than 30 feet away eating my sammy. That winged devil had swiped it. I had just found the thief. The peanut butter sandwich caper is now officially over, crime solved, and the solitary cyclist (That's me) is headed for home after depositing the remainder of a once fine supper into the trash bin.

Keep in mind what the wannabe flatfoot said previously: He's not normally observant, doesn't pay attention to most everyday activities and above all doesn't rightly care – and it showed. If the wannabe had looked in his paper bag he would have noticed both sandwiches had been pilfered. If he had glanced toward the grounds keeper, he wouldn't have accused the raven of filching his supper. No, the grounds keeper was busy savoring a peanut butter sandwich at the time, and he was likely the villain who removed both morsels and had thrown one to the bird, a very likely scenario.

Whoa, hold on a sec! The wannabe's take on this filching business might have been much different if he had all the facts. Anybody that believed Wikileaks was a bladder malfunction could decide the bird swiped both sammies and gave one to the grounds keeper.

PREFACE

History surfaces from a few chosen experts. It's unlikely the average person contributes to historical documentaries or the written word, especially young people. What would it be like to see several World War 2 incidents through the eyes of a juvenile? How does it compare to the experts' versions? Turn the page and begin your pursuit of the truth.

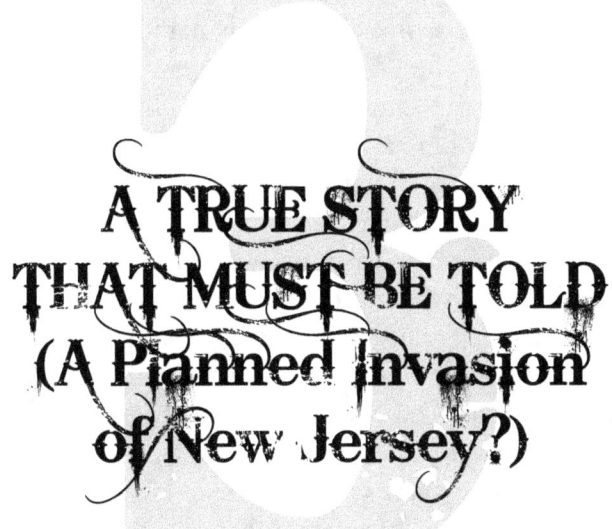

A TRUE STORY THAT MUST BE TOLD (A Planned Invasion of New Jersey?)

I think storing unforgettable events in one's mind is like blowing up a balloon, with every worthy memory comparable to one puff of air. If the analogy is correct, my balloon is surely about to burst from all the untold stories decades ago. One such story was a near calamity. Certain events remain a mystery to this day and must be told.

Little does anyone know just how close scores of individuals came to being involved in an invasion along the South Jersey Coast or perhaps territory fronting the Delaware River to include part of Pennsylvania. It would seem that certain people sitting on major stories of the day didn't want to worry folks, but wished to keep them upbeat, not let anyone think we were at considerable risk on the home front in World War II where our military preparedness was virtually nonexistent. Years later I came to realize we were as close as a gnat's hair to experiencing a real tragedy as horrific as one of the many bombings of London. Wait! I'm kind of getting ahead of myself. Let me give you a little background, followed by the actual incidents and finally how I eventually came to put the facts together after watching a documentary. The events occurred when I was a boy, not suspecting the historians had gotten it all wrong … until I reached my late seventies.

Now for the background: What were the old days like in Whale Beach, New Jersey? Well, for starters there was no running water, TV, computers, electronic games, phone service, police force or fire department. Gas cost less than 20 cents a gallon and was rationed due to the war.

This wilderness area is where I hung my hat for the summer of 1942. No one could imagine the Germans having an interest in the area so nothing changed initially. Our little family of three lived the good life. Dad had his croaker fishing across the street. Mom, being a beach person, loved every minute of living on the sea side of massive sand dunes. Actually, our house was built parallel to the lapping waves. The stage was set now for what was about to catch us by surprise in the summer of "42" in remote Whale Beach where Mom, Dad and I had a front row seat.

I was a typical, excitable seven year-old at the time and could even recognize airplanes on both sides. I had asked Santa for a wooden rifle the previous Christmas. The war in Europe seemed a little exhilarating to me so long as we were at a safe distance. Dad and Mom assured me I was out of harm's way where we lived. I read local newspapers to keep up with current events. We were safe from the bad guys from what I was told and read. German planes hadn't the range to bomb New Jersey, and we possessed a most impressive navy. People who scanned the daily rags felt pretty secure. How could they reach us? It wasn't long before I started believing more of what I saw than read. Everybody knew the enemy had an imposing submarine fleet, torpedoing everything in sight crossing the Atlantic. That same body of water nearly reached our front door. Nothing stopped them from roaming the sea right there in front of us. There were targets aplenty, long lines of ships steaming up the coastline from sunup to dusk.

Then, one day the coastguard beach patrol knocked on our front door. A pleasant young man toting a semiautomatic thirty-caliber rifle explained a few basic rules that would be enforced. Nothing seemed threatening about his demeanor, but the coastal military was explicit: black shades pulled down on all windows at night or the lights must be doused, nothing visible ocean side. After sundown, cars had to back into streets perpendicular to the ocean, and binoculars were not permitted for scanning the sea. The top half of auto headlamps had to be painted black. According to the coast guard, U-boats prefer surfacing in darkness to find their bearings for the next day's hunt. Lights on shore make their job much easier. Debris and tarred beaches proved they were successful. My Uncle Everett, a member of the Cape May Coastguard, went one further. He told us, after we promised to keep a secret, spies infiltrated Jersey Shore by submarine, and they don't pick bright moonlit nights or heavily populated regions to do it. This bit of input meant we lived in a section of coastline susceptible to enemy activity.

One morning, when Dad and I went for cinnamon buns in Sea Isle City by car, we spotted considerable commotion on the beach. The armed military had cordoned off an area around a smallish black raft on the beach. Bingo, our first spies that I knew of personally had come ashore. Uncle Everett verified the landing and said two infiltrators had successfully penetrated our shores. He sounded positive about the number and said landings were not uncommon. I figure the coast guard found two sets of footprints leading away from the raft. In the coming weeks the scuttlebutt circulating in the Sea Isle bakery sounded ominous. Not wanting to be detected, the Germans more than likely didn't have time to destroy their raft since the landing took place on a city beach, certainly not their objective. Obvious questions arose: How many other landings were there? Where did the infiltrators go? Was this the beginning of something big about to happen? If so, what was it? I kind of believed this was just the beginning when finding new fishing equipment on the beach early one morning. None of the gear was meant for surf fishing. Whoever brought it never thought to include bait. I can't believe these were the choices of a sportsman. Someone had to be posing as a fisherman and was there for devious reasons.

To me, people not allowed to search the sea with binoculars started to make sense. Since there were no telephone lines in the area, local inhabitants spotting U-boats would be of little use to the military considering the time it takes to report the incident. But, anyone found using binoculars on the beach just might be in cahoots with the enemy by trying to contact one of their subs, and since it was against regulations, they would undoubtedly be hauled into headquarters for questioning if caught. Regardless, Uncle Chester, who was visiting at the time, spotted a periscope from our front porch with his binoculars and assisted the entire household in seeing it.

I couldn't help getting worried living at the shore that year, a war was going on right in front of me. By midsummer, blimps and PT boats began dropping depth charges several hundred yards into the sea just off the beach. It seemed to me multiple explosions were heard most days and rattled dishes inside our beach house. At times the whole place shook. Detonations were getting closer. Once I happened to be standing on the beach at low tide when two blasts vibrated the ground under my feet so violently it knocked me down. I wasn't hurt. I thought it was neat, but didn't think it so great when the body of a dead German submariner washed ashore close by. Before beaching, the lifeless man bumped into Dad while we were swimming in the surf. He tried grabbing the man's shirt, but the strong undertow pulled the body back out to sea. Mom screamed and didn't go near the water for the better part of a month.

Occasionally, a periscope was spotted by beach goers, no wonder with all the shipping activity. Tankers and freighters sailed up the coast single file keeping a good distance between ships making it more difficult for subs to zero in on multiple targets. The longer the U-boat commanders remained active the more they put themselves in danger of being sunk. Ships came closer to shore causing the subs to enter shallower water where they could be seen more easily by a surface vessel or from a blimp.

Then it happened, oh God, in the middle of the night. Clunking noises under the house – something or someone banged into piling, the very pillars holding up our house. Next, the receiver of a gun rammed shut. I grew up with guns and could recognize the sound of live ammunition being slammed into position in preparation for firing. Dad tore out the back door. All went initially quiet for what seemed like a lifetime. Finally muffled voices from under the house filtered through the floorboards, Dad was clearly having a talk with someone. Not long after he returned, nervous as a squirrel watching a cat climb its tree. He told Mom and me a shocking story I'll take to my final resting place.

Mom spoke first. "Who was that you were talking to, France?" She always called Dad France.

Dad looked a little pale under the yellow light cast by a 40-watt bulb screwed into that dingy table lamp of ours. Before responding he seemed to try collecting his thoughts for a minute. "Oh, ah, he was an officer I think, in charge of the other men."

"There were others?" Mom said.

"The coast guard set up headquarters under our house," Dad said. "They have a machinegun nest down there! The other men were spread along the sand dunes."

The worst was yet to come, the real scary stuff. At dusk, a mystery ship the size of a troop carrier had been spotted by the beach patrol directly off shore from our house. But this craft wouldn't identify herself. She wasn't one of ours. All ships were required to contact the proper authorities when entering coastal waters. One good size ship could transport thousands of soldiers, and the coast guard from the Cape May base at full strength mustered less than two hundred as I remember. In those days the military had no means of tracking ships at night, this meant the guard dug in and waited, all 150 or so men.

Nothing happened. Uncle Everett informed us blimps, planes and PT boats went in search of the ship the following morning. The vessel remains a mystery to this day, never seen again.

Over time the home front war diminished then ended. As a kid of seven, I really never thought much about the incidences until my late seventies when a TV documentary failed to cover any of the events I saw and heard: spies setting foot on New Jersey beaches, submarines cruising the shoreline. There was no mention of a mystery ship – absolutely nothing.

I started thinking, speculating actually about the incidents along the Jersey Shore, the mystery ship in particular. Uncle Evert swore the vessel came from Germany. Were their intentions to kill people then depart? Hitler's bombing of London was designed to kill people. The objectives could have been much bigger. Several oil refineries, the Navy Yard and the New York Shipyard were built along the Delaware River and are accessible from the ocean, a mere sixty mile trip. Who could stop the enemy, certainly not the contingent of Cape May Coast Guard in the dark. If this were the intended mission, the ship's captain arrived too far up the coast to achieve his objective. This and the fact he was spotted I believe were the reasons he left.

It's my belief a World War II invasion of New Jersey had been thwarted, and it isn't in our history books.

INTRO

Let me introduce you to Air Hare. He's a very, very unique bunny with incredibly serious problems. Will the little tyke triumph or succumb to his trials and tribulations? Turn the page and begin your adventure.

AN AIR HARE EXCLUSIVE

Not many people have seen a rabbit with wings. This is the absolute truth. I kid you not! As a matter of fact, most living beings could care less about cute little bunnies sporting long, floppy ears, wiggling noses, and short puffy tails. But let one be a high flying cottontail and you've got instant TV coverage, a real media feeding frenzy on your hands – definitely a high profile situation. This must be avoided by the little guy.

Well, our little guy isn't made of space age stuff but does sport feathery appendages. So, where he fits into the scheme of things is anybody's guess.

By the way, did I tell you his name is Air Hare? This Hare guy has wings like I said, one on each side to be exact, although he doesn't have the teensiest clue how to use them.

Now let's get one thing straight. Just because a bun-bun sports bird gear it doesn't mean old hippity hop would take off and do the wild blue yonder bit, not until he gets a handle on things. No sir, his mamma didn't raise a fool. What would Air do with the publicity anyway? After all, he's only a rabbit. A big contract with lots of loot would mean nothing to a pint-sized ball of fur, or would it? Looks like we've got a bad case of extenuating circumstances here, whatever that means.

Of course, sooner or later, almost everybody wants to live up to his billing. You know, if you've got it, use it or at least give it your best shot and deal with the collateral damage later.

The choices most of us make in our lives are a lot more difficult than to buzz off or not to buzz off. But in this case, Air's problem is very complex. Good old Air just wants to be a normal carrot eater with an occasional lettuce leaf thrown in on alternate Sundays. However, he doesn't stand a snowball's chance in Phoenix, Arizona … not with appendages sticking out of his shoulders.

Well anyway, I'm getting ahead of myself. So, let's get back to the story. This little whippet of fur can't get along with his buddies for the long haul. Actually, they don't like him because he's different. Or maybe it's because he has something they don't. I'd say that's more likely.

His earthbound look-alikes, minus the bird equipment, tried everything to convince him not to hang out in the clouds. Besides calling him names and making fun of his wings, they attempted to scare him out of doing something they couldn't. "Learn to lift off, Air Hare, and you'll be doing time in a tree with a bunch of unfriendly crows or splashing around in a pond full of ducks, trying your best to stay afloat."

After agreeing he'd surely fall out of a tree in the first instance and break his neck or possibly drown in the second, Air kind of convinced the gullible group he would never wing it, but he didn't actually come right out and say so. Keep that in your noodle for future consideration if you will.

Every evening the little Hare guy could be seen eating outside the warren. Overlooking the affair, the Bunny Ladies Auxiliary always seemed to rail about several sore points, loud enough for all to hear, as they watched him and the other young ones munch on carrots in a small vegetable bed atop a nearby knoll. "The food here is not to my liking," complained one doe. "I agree," said another. "The lettuce is wilted. It needs watering. The ground is too hard for digging, weeds are everywhere, and you never know when that farmer's cat is going to show up." As evening wore on, their prattle would become spiteful. "Mrs. Hare, won't you pu-lease do something about those unsightly wings on your son? They're enough to spoil one's appetite. At least tie them underneath him so they're not as noticeable. We'd hate for other warrens to see our children playing with the likes of him, if you know what we mean. How could we explain away the bird feathers? We'd be plume humiliated." (No pun intended here. Rabbits you see don't have a good handle on vocabulary.)

As days slipped by their maliciousness reached new heights. Either do something about the wings or take a hike and never return pretty much described the situation. To make matters worse, Air's group of so-called friends continually badmouthed him, feeding off their mothers' biting remarks. They tried their best to cause the little rabbit lots of grief and it appeared as though they succeeded. During evening soufflés, Mrs. Hare's son looked dejected, run down from the constant harassment. The spring was gone from his hop, he never smiled and only rarely spoke. Even his appetite seemed poor. He would drag his anchor behind the others like some outcast.

No one took the time or came close enough to notice the glimmer in his eyes. In reality, Air was happy, smiling on the inside as he did his thing, big time. After careful consideration, Air Hare had decided to use the special gift he was born with, if he could.

When a man with a regular day job finds other work at night, it's called moonlighting. I don't know what you call it for sure when a rabbit carries on his normal routine at night then spends time at something else during the day when he should be sleeping. I suppose you could call it day-lighting. Yes, day-lighting sounds about right for what bun-bun was doing.

Anyway, this guy bunny of ours sneaks out of his cubbyhole every single day after all the rabbits fall sound asleep and heads for a nearby field with a fairly level dirt path running through it, a perfect place out in the boonies to get a hopping good start for takeoff. High weeds on either side of the runway keep him reasonably safe from prying eyes and of course predators.

Anxious to get off the ground once his mind had been made up, Air bypassed the mechanics of flying at first and worked on, or should I say daydreamed about his flight pattern. When I take off I'll just bank left, stay under the high-tension wires, and keep below the tree line, where nobody can spot me.

Ha! What a joke. Thinking alone doesn't get the job done, working at it does. Young Air had wings – can't dispute it – nice substantial flappers at that. But, the cottontail was no bird type. Sure, a furious hop down the dirt runway, wings beating a mile a minute, looked good, at least initially. He even managed to accomplish a successful liftoff. Unfortunately, he was unable to steer and had no idea how to control his wings for a landing. A crash was definitely in the offing. Poor little guy slammed hard into the dirt path time and time again until his body ached all over. Up til now he hadn't thought about steering or controlling his descent. He figured those abilities came naturally with the wings. However, the increasing level of pain made him rethink his game plan. It seems some research, including the finer points of winging it, was in order.

Several days pass. You could find the hare guy spending his time bird watching. Check out the experts if you want to learn how to do something was young Air's motto now. The bunny noticed birds using their tail feathers to steer. I may not have any feathers on my tail but so what?

Rabbit tails are just as good.

Armed with this vital information, it was back to the practice field. I see how it's done now. Geez, anybody with wings can do the flying bit. Hopping like mad down the dirt road, the confident bunny gained speed and lifted off. Think I'll zip left and pick up some altitude, maybe catch an upward draft or two.

Using his tail, he tries to steer left. Almost immediately, a not so soft kerplunk was followed by a scraping sound where fur met the road. As he slides to a stop, the bunny tries to solve the mystery behind his crash when a slightly misguided robin, better described as a birdbrain, lands beside him.

"Yo, kid, take it easy. Give yourself a break. You know, it's easier to launch yourself from a tree. See?" said the robin.

"But, sir, I can't even get up a tree."

"No problem, kid, just jump off that cliff over there, and all your troubles will be over."

Birdbrain was right, dead right, because the cliff drop off was a good thousand feet or so … straight down.

Now rabbits aren't stupid, but this one kinda lost sight of the real world, blinded by a desire to reach his goal without knowing anything about the one, that would be bird brain, telling him what to do and without considering all the possible consequences.

Air Hare plunged over the side with a smile on his face and a glimmer in his eye. As the bunny gained speed in a downward spiral, his smiley face evaporated along with his confidence and his eyes opened wide, the size of rabbit holes, in sheer terror.

Thoughts raced through his head as he plummeted toward the ground. He changed his mind about flying. I shouldn't have gone behind my mother's back. If I told her what I wanted to do, maybe she'd have talked me out of it. Whoops, too late now. I better get back to the business at hand. Missile boy was at least on the right track now for what good it would do him. With this last thought in mind the rabbit guy, ears plastered to his head by the rush of air and all four legs spread straight out, gathered enough strength to flap his wings harder. Hmmm, Air Hare begins to pick up more speed – just what he needed right? Unfortunately, he was on a downward flight path. Suddenly, at what seemed like mach 1, the ground was fast coming up to meet the little tyke. The rabbit wonder prepared for the impact … for what reason is anybody's guess. Nevertheless, he lifted his head, arched his back, and adjusted his four trembling tootsies to curve like his back. A few might say the Hare guy experienced some kind of a gut reaction. Others would say with equal certainty, he didn't have a clue to what was about to happen. Which ever side you take one thing is perfectly clear. A miracle took place that day. By the way he bent his body Air pulled out of the dive and successfully flew over treetops. Bun-bun had learned to spread his wonderful wings and fly.

Though eating worms was out of the question, Air became fast friends with birdbrain, was idolized by the bunny community and lived happily ever after. This proves it's important to work with what you've got … even if it's wings.

Story 5

Beware!

Unlit streets and the darkest alleys are where the Phantom of Sasebo resides. No one has ever seen his face. No one wants to get that close. Let a nineteen year old soldier be your guide, and … don't freak out on me. To learn more, turn the page.

Phantom of Sasebo

An adventure I lived as a nineteen year old army sergeant will remain a mystery to me until the day I die, and the lead up to it won't be forgotten either. Hostilities in Korea had abruptly ended in 1953, and my unit was shipped off to Sasebo, Japan, a thriving seaport. Why the army brass made this decision remained a puzzle to many but not to me. One day I was in Mig Alley and the next, piling into a landing craft and being transported to Japan. I suspected the general in charge felt sorry for my unit due to the awful food impositions we suffered through. We had received a shipment where the meat refrigeration compartments had fizzled out on an old supply vessel during its crossing of the Pacific, and the grub putrefied. This is true. Regardless, the smelly, decayed maggot attraction was delivered to us anyway. This greenish looking crap, I couldn't call it meat, was actually cooked and served once. That's all the supposed fresh meat we had at the time, our monthly supply no less. Not only was the color disgusting, but I couldn't get it passed my nose it stunk so badly. Of course, nobody ate the slop. Instead, my unit gagged on the backup garbage provided, World War 1 canned C rations – yuck. I suspect many of that war's casualties were attributable to the swill they were served in the trenches.

Anyway, I ended up stationed in downtown Sasebo Compound – not bad. The army food there, however, was nauseating, too. For a minute it seemed as though I was back in Korea, but the meat wasn't green. I ate as many noonday meals as I could afford in downtown Sasebo. Compared to the compound slop, this was culinary heaven. Poached succulent prawns were two to a pound, and steaks were nearly as tender as ground meat. There was a problem though. Ever try eating a Porterhouse with chopsticks?

You might say lunch time was where my adventure began, when overhearing several navy wives talking about a predator, the Phantom of Sasebo. "Don't leave the well-lit areas after dark, Martha," one said. Another added, "My husband's buddy vanished several weeks ago. The navy listed him as AWOL. We're sure the Phantom got him." This scuttlebutt happened to be the first time I heard about this Phantom guy.

Returning to the compound I decided to enter into a conversation with one of the two gate guards, a Sasebo native. He spoke perfect English. We finally got around to him chatting on about that Phantom person. I learned a lot. No one ever saw his face or knew his identity, pretty much the reason for his given moniker, Phantom of Sasebo. As the story goes, he was likely an old retired Japanese army veteran and responsible for many dastardly deeds, possibly murder. The locals as well as Americans should keep alert. Warnings were issued: Most importantly, never venture into less frequented places in town, especially the residential sections at night. Street lighting was between poor to nonexistent in places, quite likely the reason nobody ever saw his face. I might add, and lived to tell about it. Oh, yes, and the scoundrel put food on his table by breaking into homes and stealing from the citizenry of Sasebo, mostly those working for the U.S. military. I often wondered how this phantom being ever knew which ones to rob. Who told him? I can't believe he picked up the pertinent information by himself. People would remember his scarred face.

Oops, there I go jumping ahead in the story. Sorry!

One other tidbit I would like to share: Why weren't the police patrolling the residential areas the Sasebo Phantom cruised at night? I didn't see any when I needed them. Oh geez, there I go again jumping ahead of myself.

Before giving the best parts away, it's time to soar headlong into the mashed potatoes and gravy of my adventure. People in the compound suggested newcomers take a trip to the top of Sasebo Hill. Views from the cliff were considered spectacular. So, I made the jaunt one late Sunday afternoon. Traveling the winding road up by taxi was an adventure in itself. Streets had no stop signs. Screeching tires and blowing horns were the norm for such trips. The first horn to wail had the right of way most times, and bicycles were fair game. I often wondered what happened if two cars honked at the same time.

The enjoyable view was worth the excursion, but … I couldn't understand why there were so few people in a place so beautiful and so highly recommended. It should have been crowded. Vendor stands were closed tighter than a miser's wallet. What's wrong here? Is it Phantom related?

Looking around, I noticed no taxis had pulled in lately. My only conveyance back was apparently done for the evening, a mistake I would soon regret. The sun started to slip below the horizon, still no sign of a taxi. People began quick stepping down Sasebo Hill Road with an urgent look scrawled across their faces. Obviously, they lived close by and wanted to get home. The uncertainties of night were approaching. This wasn't a good place to be after dark.

I turned to the remaining couple and tried communicating, "Is anything wrong?"

"No speaka Engla" was the woman's response or something like that. Then she quickly shuffled off.

I didn't like the looks of her partner, the unnaturally pleasant smile etched into his face. He nodded, mumbling in Japanese. I suppose he wasn't so bad. It was just me getting hyper over the darkness settling in and being confronted with a several hour walk through vast residential areas in the murky shadows of night, the Phantom's home turf. In minutes I was alone, standing on a 1500 foot over-look.

Within a quarter hour's walk a mist rolled in from the Sea of Japan and hugged the hill. Night turned pitch black. I couldn't see the road I walked on at times. Dim street lamps spaced hundreds of yards apart left large swaths void of light. Not all straightaways between the many bends in the road even had streetlamps. I knew from my army boots clunking on the cobblestone street that I hadn't wandered off track, and so could anybody else within hundreds of feet of the noise.

Well into the stroll my heart skipped several beats when noticing a man behind me through the haze. As I turned into a curve, he had burst into the light on the straightaway I just left. This man was smallish and quiet as a cat stalking his prey. Soon, I came to realize he was much closer even though I had quickened my pace. Downtown Sasebo must be at least a mile ahead. Now, he was a mere 50 feet away. At this rate he should catch up soon. Were any of his cohorts lying in wait up ahead? The thought had crossed my mind; although, I saw no one in this blackest of nights. Of course there was always a chance he could turn out to be friendly and just wanted to talk on the long trek downhill.

I took a deep breath, stopped, turned and confronted him as he stepped under a street lamp and froze. His face was badly scarred. The man's actions didn't appear to be amiable, and his abrupt halt settled the issue. He wasn't interested in catching up for a friendly chat. When he slid one hand into his jacket, I moved in his direction. Immediately, he turned and slipped into a side alley with fewer lights. I followed through thickening mist, not really wanting to catch up just make him think twice about pursuing me. He paused on a corner, checked to see if I were coming then turned left into another alley. He repeated the maneuver several more times under street lights and only turned into an alley after he caught my attention. I came to realize this. Was I being lured? For his next gambit, he stole into a back alley void of light. I couldn't see much beyond my nose and lost interest in dogging him, when recalling stories told about the villain. Being the fastest runner in my high school, I put my God given talents to good use and left in a hurry before getting lost in the maze of streets and alleys. He simply had to be the treacherous, wily Phantom of Sasebo.

Staying late at the office the next evening, I couldn't help overhearing one of the cleaning men excitedly talking to the commanding officer of the compound as they stood by the front door. He had an encounter with the Phantom of Sasebo the previous night just like I had and barely escaped from the thug in an unlit alley according to the smallish man.

Curious now, I couldn't help gawking at the wrinkled face. Wrinkles could have been mistaken for scars under poor lighting conditions. He kind of resembled the man I had chased through the back alleys last night. I just might have been his Phantom of Sasebo and he mine.

Story 6

INTRO

Do two extraordinarily outlandish people have what it takes to become … well, let's say unorthodox detectives? Can scruffy looking Vanilla and her sidekick, the unkempt rotund Codger, deal with the hazards of the occupation? Are they hazards or something more sinister? Turn the page and begin your quest to learn the answers.

Murder Knocks Twice

The story begins in a very odd way, but it must be told. Vanilla, an aging, buxom, bleach job, with hair the color and texture of straw passed through a cow at least once, resides in a middle class neighborhood on the north side of Kalispell. She lost a husband ten years ago. It wasn't on purpose according to her. As the tale goes, hubby had a habit of performing odd jobs about town in his dress-ups, such as fixing coal furnaces, replacing water lines, you name it. The dirtier the job the better he liked it. Since she did the wash, no one blamed Vanilla for carting him off one day to a department store to look for a sale on knock-around duds. That's when she came home without him.

He'd skipped out on her, and was she pissed. The woman informed missing persons, told them more than was necessary about her hubby, George. He was only good for one thing, and she couldn't figure out what that was. Vanilla made it perfectly clear, that if somebody happens to dredge up the skunk, keep him. He'd even lifted her diamond ring and wallet the night before. She had earned the money slinging hash to pay for the rock.

Following her loss, one might conclude she wasn't exactly bereaved, or whatever you'd feel after losing a husband in a department store. On the contrary, soon after his disappearance and their divorce her wealthy mom took up residence with old Saint Peter leaving Vanilla well off, a fortune to be exact. When she got over mom's death, Vanilla started smiling a lot, didn't have a care in the world … until the events.

Codger, a confirmed bachelor and a major part of this story, lives down the street not more than a grenade lob away. A good part of his life had been spent in the army, shining boots and spitting out foxhole dirt. The man hung up his army skivvies about the time of the Beatle invasion. Guess that accounts for the hippy butt length appendage protruding from the back of old Codger's head, commonly known as a ponytail in some circles. The ex-Sergeant 1st Class is never seen without a dingy fatigue hat flattened over the top of his skull. This gives his chubby jowls and small upper head the look of an upside down teacup and saucer. Rounding out his attire, Codger sports an unbuttoned fatigue shirt that shows off his greasy burger and fries stained once white tee shirt. Stretched to the limit, the material cradles his portly belly, giving him a medicine ball waistline. Any way you view it, the overall effect is striking … as in three strikes and you're out! Basically he's a slob. Get the picture?

Now, down to the meat in the soup, the peas in the pod or whatever floats your dinghy. Vanilla and Codger haven't exactly been strangers over the past couple of years. On occasion, she drops by to see him, giving the local hens something to cluck about. Before leaving his house she musses her hair, smears her lipstick, puts on a smile and lets that old cackling hen, Martha Gibson, across the street, get an eyeful from behind her see-through venetian blinds. They were always tilted in the front windows, angled for snooping. Mind you, disheveled tresses are of no bother to Vanilla. She always picks visiting Codger right before she plans to wash the rat's nest anyway. By the way, she too is a slob.

Vanilla usually happens by to borrow one or two dog-eared detective novels from Codger's vast collection. She calls them gumshoe fairytales. Neither one can stop yakking about their paperback heroes. Crazy over Sherlock Holmes, Codger always wishes he'd been born holding a magnifying glass in his hand, although that kind of a birth would've been tough on his momma. When Vanilla hears this for the first time, she tells him he just might be a certain English dude in disguise. He laughs. She likes to daydream about the two of them becoming detectives. One day they will search for an arch villain like Dr. Moriarty. She figures her friend will love the idea, eat it for breakfast, lunch and dinner, which is exactly what she offered him today – the dinner part. She saw an article in the local rag on how to break into the detective business and wants to chew it over with him. It never happens.

"I'm intuitive you know, a real Miss Marple type in the making. Remember 'A Murder Is Announced? ' "

"You got it wrong, Vanilla. It's 'Murder Is Announced. ' "

"Whatever," she says, avoiding a confrontation. "I solved the case right off. I can spot bad guys straightaway. It's my sixth sense. I'm just like her, and Kalispell is my St. Mary Mead. Believe me, I've seen everything here worth seeing, Codge Baby."

"You didn't even git the title right. How can you expect me to believe you solved the murder?" he says laughingly, "and stop callin' me Codge Baby. I hate that moniker."

"Go to hell, Codge Baby!" She did get the title right, and she knows it.

Vanilla has spaghetti boiling in the pot after sundown when she hears someone knock twice on the front door. The second knock rattles the glass and scares her tabby cat, Stinkpot. "Hold your shorts on, I'll be there in a jiffy," she shouts, a little perturbed as she hurries to the door, retying her skimpy white apron in back. "Damn thing's always coming undone." She lifts her head and peers out of the curtains. "Whoever it was took off, Kitty."

Later, Codger comes by all decked out in his Sunday finest: clean, drip-dry fatigues breaking the Guinness Book of Records for wrinkles, matching hat and near spotless tee shirt, grease stains mere shadows of the original splotches.

Vanilla isn't exactly a 5th Ave. clotheshorse herself, shoehorned into badly faded black Bermuda shorts several sizes too small, a red pinstripe Phillies baseball shirt with the name Ashburn and number one on back, topped off by a red peaked cap sporting a white P. Lord knows why she wore those duds in cooler weather and pulled the hat down backwards to boot, covering her disgusting tresses.

Codger gobbles spaghetti – fork clutched tightly in his fist – and adds to the growing collection of past meals on the front of his tee shirt. Vanilla sits awhile and waits for him to remark about how she is dressed, but he doesn't. The rotund man has other ideas.

"I remember Whitey Ashburn. He's rabbit quick. Can catch a bunny goin' to first, gut the little fuzz ball and have it ready for dinner by the time he crosses home plate." Codger was in the middle of a belly splitting laugh, enjoying his own tall tale, when someone knocks twice on the front door, irritating the hell out of Vanilla.

She answers, but nobody is there. "This is the second time I got stood up at the damned door today. The first time, I thought you forgot something and ran back home, so I left the door unlocked." All this sounds ominous.

"Nope, twasn't me, momma. Now mind you, Vanilla, I'm not preachin' to ya, but don't be leavin' the door unlocked like you do so often. Some strange things been happenin' round here lately, startin' with knockin' at the door. Earlier this evenin' two houses down from me, Jackie Brandon

– a good lookin' piece of jailbait – had some trouble. When she answered a knock at the front door, nobody was there. With her momma being in the hospital, she was alone. It happened a couple more times. So … she called me of all people, thought I was a detective. Course I told her the truth. I was just in the hopin'-to-be stage."

"Ring her up right now! Tell her we'll be there first thing in the a.m. It might be nothing, but my intuition is shouting MURDER. Better yet, she's gotta sleep someplace else tonight. With my intuitive instincts, I'd make a great detective wouldn't I, Codger?"

"Ah, um, my exact thoughts, Vanilla." Of course he was lying.

After fumbling through the phone book for her number, Codger made the call. Jackie would stay at her married sister's place for the night.

"Well, Codger, looks like this is our first case."

"Sure does. I'm gonna look under all the stones."

"Leave no stones unturned is the expression, Codger."

"Yeah, that too."

The minute Codger departs, Vanilla heads for the oak coffee table to pick up the mail she'd tossed there earlier, then flops onto the sofa. Stinkpot snuggles in beside her. "Oh, oh, Stinkpot, my innards tell me to beware. That knocking on my door earlier had to be a forewarning. Murder knocks twice I'm thinking; although, I don't want to look like a fly avoiding a flyswatter over one of my hunches if I'm wrong. Codger would never let me forget it, so I'm not calling him … just yet. Maybe I ought to empty a shelf in the pantry right above the canned peaches, where I can sleep the night away. Bad guys wouldn't look for me there, eight feet off the floor. What do you think, Stinkpot?"

"Meow."

"That's easy for you to say, cat."

Turns out Vanilla didn't sleep for most of the night. That wooden shelf she laid on was plumb uncomfortable, causing her to ache all over. Towards morning she began talking to Kitty who suddenly sat up wide-eyed at her feet. "Pull yourself together, Stinkpot," she mumbles. "Why are you so jittery, hear a noise? Oh, no. Think I just did, too. I'll lay here quiet like a rat in a grain silo and – oops! There goes my sixth sense kicking in, telling me something's mighty wrong. Ouch! My rotten back is so sore it's going to bust in half if I don't get out of here mighty soon, and I also have to pee real bad … just my luck. I'll cross my legs. Nah, that's not working. Heck with it, noise be damned! Coming, Stinkpot?"

After relieving her entrails, as she so delicately put it, Vanilla exits the downstairs john dragging a strip of toilet paper behind her and heads for the pitch-black steps, determined to scout around. "Sounds like somebody creeping down the stairs, Kitty. Oh crap! He's got a gun!" She sees the silhouette of a pistol framed in the upstairs window.

"Hi, Vanilla. How ya hittin' 'em today?"

"Codger! What're you doing in my house? It's the middle of the night!"

"No it ain't. It's 5a.m.," he says, flicking the hall light switch on.

"You got some tall explaining to do, you old bugger! Make it fast, and make it good!"

"I'll have at it over a cup of java, if you don't mind, Vanilla."

"I do mind. My ticker was doing a tap dance in my chest, and I nearly peed myself. Out with it … NOW!"

"I'm keepin' my trap shut, ain't sayin' nothin' til I've had my java, and that's final!" Codger was downright belligerent. His cantankerous streak was showing.

Vanilla gives in and heads toward the kitchen looking disgusted, eying the ceiling. Determined as a raging bull, she didn't usually surrender to anybody, but figured Codger was even more resolute, as unstoppable as a class five hurricane. "Oh, well, what the hell," she says, loud enough for him to hear.

Later, as Codger nibbles away at a piece of toast after polishing off four thick slices of fried Taylor's Ham imported from the East Coast, washed down with a second cup of coffee, and the remnants of food slopped on his shirt had formed stain blotches reminiscent of the Milky Way, he finally gets around to explaining.

"Well, it's like this, Sweet Cheeks. I'd fallen asleep on the sofa next to my front door, listenin' to my favorite tunes. Now mind ya I don't know why, just one of those things, but I came to sudden like. My Sherlock Holmes instincts told me to look out my side window. Your front door was flappin' in the autumn breeze. That hunk of wood was as wide open as my mouth when I shovel in your spaghetti, if you catch my drift. Why'd you leave it unlocked, let alone open? Expectin' visitors? Anyhow, I slipped in lookin' for the worst, prepared to save your frozen fat rump! Now you got some answerin' to do, bout that open door, invitin' the whole neighborhood in includin' any murderers passin' by, if they were of a mind ta call on ya."

"Well, my front door wasn't left open, flapping in the breeze as you put it. Hasn't been since my husband lived here. He used to leave it open even in cold weather like last night. Guess I just didn't shut it tight. That's different from leaving it flapping. Lord only knows there are times I forget to lock the blasted thing though. It was awful nice of you to be laying your life on the line for me, you being prepared to shoot it out with a burglar if need be."

"You got it all wrong, lady. I lied before bout savin' your worthless carcass. Knowin' the likes of you, I was prepared to shoot you to protect the poor man," he says, unable to conceal a little chuckle before continuing. "Even a murderer doesn't deserve your mouthin' him to death."

"Whatever you say, Codge Baby, but I still believe a killer is knocking twice. I can feel it in my bones."

"Makes sense to me, too," he says. "I got the same feelin' you do. We can't both be wrong."

Or can they? Vanilla turns the radio on, wanting to see if any murders were committed recently. Instead, she learns last night had been mischief night and a very likely reason for the knocking.

There hadn't even been any murders attempted. One might think this whole affair was a waste of time. Well … Codger didn't think so. He'd had a spaghetti supper, a scrumptious breakfast and an opportunity to add stains to his not so white tee-shirt.

Story 7

INTRO

There has to be a good reason for widespread, irrational behavior. Turn the page, learn for yourself and please don't hold the writer accountable for the initial nonsensical scribbling. He actually likes all politicians and the news media ... about as much as his wife does.

The Beginning

To tell the truth, I am an unknown storyteller, a new kid on the block. Don't confuse me with a politician, those rascals with silver tongues that sound like bards of old. You might confuse me, however, with the media that claims to report the news, you know, the so called fake news bunch. Lack of facts never stops them or me. I'm taking the fifth right now before starting my tale and hoping I'm not unmasked. By the way, the story you are about to read is true but unverified. It comes from an unknown source. The reader will have a choice of endings, different strokes for different blokes. I'll explain later.

Now let's get down to the Taylors Ham on toast, the egg in the beer or whatever sends your hot air balloon skyward. Hang on to your gotchies partners. Here we go.

Something is dead wrong. Townies stroll through the park for the last time. A fisherman wades in a posted stream. A few hunters scour fields and woods for game … even though hunting season isn't in. On closer inspection some hunters have no ammo.

Banks aren't open for business. Schools lie unattended. Unlike the two, food stores are frequented regularly by the citizenry. From time to time most people wander in, take needed provisions and leave. There are no cashiers, no clerks or managers. Selections and quantities dwindle. Most local business people leave their establishments to the whims of the public, even gas station owners. "Come in and take whatever you need, whatever you want." This seems to be the prevailing attitude.

Most of the Wednesday afternoon activity centers around two churches. At times religious tunes spring from within. Standing room congregations hang on every word spoken from the pulpit. Profound messages dwell on comforting the dejected, the overwhelmed. This smallish Midwestern town appears devastated. It looks like the grim reaper is about to swing his sickle, cutting down those from all walks of life, sparing none.

Years ago the scientific community sent a probe to a rocky planet in a nearby solar system some five plus light years away. This distance translates into more than 35 trillion miles, a gob of spittle in the ocean of cosmological distances, but a monumental undertaking for humankind. The probe had been programed to pinpoint potential landing sights. This mission was deemed successful and eventually became extremely important.

Several dozen miles beyond town an interplanetary airport was hastily constructed in secret the last few months. The present emergency created the need to transport a chosen few out of harm's way. Civilization faces complete annihilation. The twenty craft built for the mission are newly designed for the venture. Sleek winged transports will fly into orbit using the latest conventional technology in addition to hefty rocket boosters. Upon achieving orbit a matter/antimatter combustion chamber will propel craft to their one-way destination, the heavily scrutinized planet that orbits a much larger star. The trip should take roughly ten years. Twenty people per ship will remain in suspended animation for the journey.

The latest departure time according to government scientists is in three days, causing crews to hastily prepare for flight. Postponements are death sentences. A rogue exoplanet, more than likely ejected from a neighboring solar system and discovered by the astronomy community, entered the solar system hundreds of years ago. Mathematicians determined the planet to be headed our way and a collision inevitable.

Captain Adam will pilot one ship. He and his crew actually helped built the craft. They will be taking their wives on the voyage. The intent is to repopulate another planet. The human race must prevail. This is their only chance.

Early the next day the captain calls a meeting and brings the travelers together in their barracks.

"We are taking off now not tomorrow as originally planned. Grab your belongings and follow me." The captain didn't like the looks of the morning sky. It was deep red as usual, but constant flecks of lightening could be a forewarning. The rogue planet, taking up a good part of the eastern sky, also unnerves him. Yesterday, catastrophic events struck the world's coastal regions. Thousand foot waves washed hundreds of miles inland wiping out 80% of the world's population. The planet's gravitational pull was obviously responsible. Captain Adam is afraid that same pull might crack his planet's mantel and inundate the world with sizzling molten rock and deadly toxic fumes. Wasting little time the twenty people are on their way: blasting off, orbiting and setting course for their destination, the rocky planet.

Captain Adam feels saddened and relieved after departing. In a matter of days the rogue planet will collide with his beloved world according to the experts.

He speaks through the intercom. "Ladies and gentlemen it is now time for you to lay back and enter into suspended animation. Good luck!"

Ready for the long haul, he glances to the rear and sees the other nineteen people looking reassured as they prepare for the next ten years. Previously successful dry runs had obviously built their confidence. Satisfied the trip is going smoothly, he peers toward the planet for the final time. "It can't be," he says to himself. Deadly cracks appear below, spewing molten rock thousands of feet into the air. Most of the other pilots had decided to leave tomorrow. In near shock, Captain Adam activates the suspended animation system then joins his wife in the longest snooze of his life.

At first it seems as though something went wrong as he and his cohorts recover from a deep sleep. It feels to him as though the ship never set course for their destination. Upon entering the cockpit a magnificent blue planet comes into view. The trip is practically over, how nice. "We made it! We're here!"

Spotting a pine cone shaped continent, he grabs the controls and heads for the beautiful upper northern quadrant, locates grasslands and prepares for a landing to the east side of the only lake in the region.

"Get your seat belts on folks and bend forward."

They do as told. The ship lands wheels up and skids to a sudden stop. In good spirits, the little group piles out and begins to talk amongst themselves. Captain Adam's booming voice comes across as the easiest to hear.

"YOU OKAY, EVE?"

"Yes my darling husband."

"AND WHAT SHOULD WE NAME OUR NEW HOME?"

After careful consideration she smiles and responds. "This will be known as the Garden of Eden and our new home shall be called Earth! Our first two children will be boys."

"Yes, Eve, and they shall be named Cain and Abel."

STOP! HOLD IT! This is your wily storyteller speaking once more. I have a second ending for your perusal. Please read this version and decide which one lights your fire or … as the case may be, scrambles your eggs. Personally, I relate to the second one and almost believe it's true. I'll explain later. Now buckle up, here we go again. Captain Adam had already taken off.

Before his deep sleep the captain ponders over the enormity of their mission. The most powerful telescopes in the world and probes assured him life exists on the new planet. However, there was no way to determine how far living creatures had evolved or what they've become. Based on gathered evidence, the experts concluded intelligent beings are nonexistent, even though strange radio signals were detected spewing from the planet. As a whole, the scientific community decided the origin of the signals had to be occurring quite naturally, not man made. It almost sounded like herds of animals passing gas, a perfect description of the news prognosticators giving their version of the news. About then the captain falls into his deep ten year sleep beside his wife. He looks comfortable and at peace with the turbulent times.

It seems like a matter of seconds when all twenty people regain consciousness and become aware they had just successfully landed in a dark new world. The black of night closes in on them. Afraid something might be lurking unseen nearby that heard the little band land, Captain Adam issues a command.

"Time to leave. Let's move out."

Eyes adjusting to a never before seen penetrating darkness, the group cradles their meager belongings in their arms and descends into the black abyss one by one. Captain Adam leads the way. At first, threatening leafy trees overhang a forest trail. Branches poised to pounce, the wary captain moves forward unfalteringly. A slight breeze seems to stir the larger limbs into life and rattle twigs and leaves in the doing. Wind blowing through the forest creates a soothing, whistling sound. In time the forest symphony of woodsy tunes projects a calming effect. The trekkers begin to relax in their new surroundings. A few break into nervous giggles, not completely convinced all is well. The few keep a lookout for flesh-eating carnivores.

"I see an opening ahead, STOP!" Captain Adam commands. "We'll stay here until dawn. Now let's gather along the tree line, eat our food pills and keep vigilant, OK?"

Everyone agrees, and they do as told. Soon the sky lightens enough for a paved street to appear. Night continues its retreat. Structures loom in the waning darkness. Finally, a business district materializes beyond the street. As the sun chases the final flecks of darkness, hoards of people advance in their direction, bearing signs. It's hard to comprehend, but the placards are in English. The creatures seem harmless enough. Captain Adam tries to read the messages while the mob chants senseless slogans he doesn't understand.

"Down with the constitution. Illegals should have voting rights. Why can't churches provide condoms? Three public bathrooms have to become the law. I should be able to marry a bug if I decide to. I want free college tuition. It's my right as an illegal."

The captain turns to his wife. "From what I've seen, our scientists were spot on about this planet. There is life here … but no signs of intelligent life."

Story 8

Preface

Did you ever think you heard sinister sounds while sleeping? Abraham does! Are they real? A dream? Turn the page and begin your pursuit for a resolution that might shake your under-pinnings a bit and perhaps set you straight.

Uncommon Sounds

Strange sounds invade the very air Abraham inhales. "Somebody help me! Please help before it's too late!" he says, choking on his final words. In a drenching sweat he fights to rise from a troubled sleep. A barrage of unfriendly chatter and eerie wailing respond to his pleas in the din of predawn morning. Waves of evil presence creep closer, so close he smells their rancid odors.

Abraham struggles to gain consciousness. Finally he awakens, but barely in the nick of time. All the intimidating prattle surrounding him instantly ceases, along with those reeking smells. Was it all a dream, a partial dream or a living nightmare? Seen through a bedroom window, the outside appears brighter to him for a few seconds, but why?

This wasn't the first assault. The events grow worse, more frightening. These episodes feel real. There is an assumed degree of uncertainty; still, deep down, he believes he had escaped from something dreadful.

"Let us suppose it is happening," he says. Being vulnerable, the young man has taken to chatting to himself. "I feel threatened with these likely hideous forces of evil, and where did they go so quickly? Wait … I have an idea this time," he says, remembering the brightness outside.

Leaping out of bed, he bare-foots it to the front window of his dilapidated two room shack. Abraham spots what appears to be a brilliant ball of white light moving through the woods. It quickly fades from sight before he gets a good look. Is this somehow related to the incident? "Yes," he declares. "I'm sure of it … well, not positive."

After the sun climbs above trees to the east of his farm, Abraham sets out to investigate a forest he and his father had never dared to explore. He tries to calm his nerves: "That ball of light could have been a lantern. If so, someone must have left footprints on the woodland path, since rain showers had softened the ground earlier." Turns out, there were no footprints or any other indentations except his and old wagon wheel ruts from yesteryears. These findings were kind of anticipated and further convinced him the ball of light is really after him. With this in mind and a little scared, he takes off running back home.

Decisions must be made. How can evil forces be stopped, assuming they exist? First, locate them. Learn more about them but be careful, very careful. This will require entering a forest his father once told him to avoid. The idea unnerves him. Nobody ever frequents this mysterious region, for good reason. His dad never did fully explain the rationale behind such a negative outlook but went on to paint a bleak mental picture of a hamlet.

What's left of remaining paths and roads were established by pre-World War I pioneers of long ago. As the story goes, the pioneers suddenly went missing from the hamlet and were never heard from again. No one ever dared to investigate, since the place had such a bizarre reputation. He would be the first to venture in.

To begin his lengthy trek, Abraham will take the path the white light used and continue on until discovering the little hamlet, provided the path leads to the settlement. He has no other options. His response is focused on coping with recent developments and making the best decisions. The unthinkable alternative is to avoid the light by abandoning his little farm, or so he believes. The man is convinced his course of action is the correct one, the only one for him since he depends upon his land – planting crops to sell and for his own consumption. It takes him most of the day to muster up courage.

This is not the best time of day or year to begin a lengthy trek. Ice is beginning to form on the river edges close by, a sure sign of coming winter. It won't be long before it freezes over. The drop in temperature usually triggers snow storms. Keeping all this in mind, he decides to shove off anyway with food in his backpack, a small six pack of bottled water, a winter sleeping bag, dad's old double barrel shotgun and a deep concern imbedded across his brow.

An overhead umbrella of intertwined evergreens forms a narrow, gloomy passageway through the forest as thick clouds block out the sun, making his trek even more dismal. Abraham doesn't own a compass, never needed one until now, and he can't determine his direction by using the sun. Under present circumstances, he must remain on the easy to follow but foreboding trail or become hopelessly lost in the deep, dark woods.

"I can only pray I don't meet up with that ball of light, a bear or anything else capable of forcing me to leave the trail."

Well into his trek the path splits. The bigger one veers left, the other right. Both have wagon wheel ruts. Difference in size makes his decision easy – stay the course by keeping to the bigger path. Several dreary hours finally pass as night approaches. Now storm clouds assemble overhead. The sky darkens even more. A clap of thunder rolls through the woodlands leaving him a bit spooked.

"Thank heavens it's not about to snow. It's too warm," he says, feeling relieved by embracing the positive side. "Everything will be okay."

Not true! A speck of light appears to be slicing through the darkening woods on a collision course with him. Abraham spots a log cabin just off the path. He breaks into a run hoping to reach the building unnoticed. Slipping behind the dilapidated structure keeps him well hidden from a likely adversary. The sky's dimming brightness concludes the bright light's silent passing. He exhales in relief.

"I didn't hear anyone walking. But … that doesn't mean it wasn't a person. Most people I know would never think of hiking around here though." Abraham stops to think for a minute. "Guess it's getting too dark to go on. So, I might as well stay here for the night."

The cabin is obviously beyond repair and uninhabited. However, the dwelling is usable for a sleepover. A clap of thunder brings rain. A steady drizzle drips through the porous roof. Abraham finds a dry closet, shuts the door, turns on a portable light and eats supper before hitting his sleeping bag for the night. Feeling perfectly secure, he promptly falls into a deep sleep and peacefully dreams the night away.

Morning comes quickly, and Abraham is up at the break of dawn. The man sits on the floor, ravenously eating a breakfast of fruit and several sandwiches while scanning his surroundings. There's a fireplace, a loft, old wood burning stove and a few eating utensils on the kitchen table.

"Whoever lived here evidently left in a hurry." The first thing that came to mind was the ball of white light. "I wonder if it scared them badly enough, like it did me, to leave some of their stuff behind. On second thought, maybe a forest fire caused their quick exit."

When departing, Abraham notices a horse stable for the first time and wagon wheel ruts leading into the main path. The ruts only turn right. The main path he took here abruptly ends. Apparently it exists as a way of getting to the cabin, not the hamlet. Once again Abraham must deal with a cloudy sky. Not wanting to get lost, he decides to head for home.

On the way, his thoughts turn to the previous cabin inhabitants leaving behind their kitchen utensils and the wood burning stove. "They must have been desperate." With this in mind, Abraham bypasses his shack and goes to a buddy's place a half mile down the road. His friend, Ichabod, hadn't experienced any white light problems. "Well, I'm not staying at home until I learn more about that ball of light."

Being good pals, Ichabod welcomes his lifelong buddy. "Stay as long as you like Abe."

Snow starts falling the next day and keeps coming. Accumulations make traveling in the back country impossible. This frustrates Abraham. Not much to do, he and Ichabod while-away the days playing video games and ice skating on a nice pond down the plowed road. One month of doing the same things day in and day out becomes boring for Abraham. When Ichabod visits his married sister for a day, he decides to skate up the iced over river. This is something new. With a backpack full of sandwiches, bottles of water and boots he takes off, working his way up river to see how far he can go.

An hour and a half of rigorous skating and he becomes pooped, time to stop. The workout brings on pangs of hunger. To his right, a fallen tree provides perfect accommodations for a famished skater to sit and enjoy his lunch, so he does.

Finished eating, recuperating and about to head back, Abraham notices a building across the river ice. The structure is covered in vines. Well hidden, he nearly missed seeing it. Discoveries always stir his anticipation. Speed skating to the other side brings him to the building. A wooden axle juts out the back wall. This intrigues him further. Changing into his boots, he proceeds to take one step into a dilapidated shack. It's falling apart. Walls collapsing and roof caving in, the man can't continue. He doesn't have to. This was once a mil for producing flour. The grinding stones are still in place. That wooden axle protruding through the wall is the remains of a paddle wheel once used to supply power to grind wheat.

Exiting the building Abraham looks straight ahead. He can visualize where a little settlement once stood. What had been a street was replaced by a forest. Amongst trees, two rows of demolished shacks are visible on each side of the envisioned street.

As he investigates further, an idea pops into his head. "This has to be the little hamlet I was looking for – great!" Searching through debris he finds several rusted wood burning stoves, a few drinking glasses and a couple broken dishes in pockets of rubble. "Just as I thought, these pioneers left in a hurry; although, they seem to have taken most of their personnel items and essentials capable of being hauled in a horse drawn wagon." The scene before him doesn't place people in a panic mode as though a ball of white light scared them into considering immediate action. It would seem they took time to load up their wagons in preparation for escaping an advancing forest fire. Abraham felt sure of this until he stumbles upon their community center. A framed map still hangs on a crumbling wall with a handwritten note attached to it. "They want everything!" This was likely discussed in a town meeting, he decides. The map of the area extends to and includes his farm. Did the word "they" refer to the white ball of light?" Abraham couldn't help wondering.

The sun perches on a snow capped mountain to the west. Darkness will soon be coming – time to leave. Shadows pop up everywhere, creating convenient hiding places for lurking evil doers. The man isn't a coward or a fool to be sure, so he leaves shortly. Moon and snow light the sky and surroundings. From time to time he glances behind him. No one follows. Abraham feels uneasy as though he is being watched. He felt the same way back there. If true, will a ball of light take revenge on him for entering its domain? According to his dad, nobody ever looked into the hamlet where people supposedly vanished. He was the first. Were they afraid to investigate? Maybe they didn't want to place themselves in jeopardy like he just did. This thought makes him nervous, a bit squeamish. He has no weapon. His dad's loaded shotgun stands in a corner by the front door of his shack.

Returning home, Abraham tosses his ice skates on the floor and prepares to head for his buddy's place. For some reason he recalls the rancid odor that filled his nostrils in what he finally decided was a dream. Startled at the thought, he freezes in the doorway for several seconds before hearing a barrage of chatter and wailing. The noises come from a white ball of light descending through the trees.

Ichabod likes to tell the story of his friend's run-in with a mysterious white ball of light. He starts with the nightmares it caused, then the trip to the hamlet and finishes with a final encounter. "Was he about to confront one of them there confounded UFO things?" Ichabod says, in a raised voice. "Or … was it something even more sinister?" he whispers.

"Abraham just grabbed the old shotgun by the door when he spied that baffling nemesis of his and blew its lights out. In seconds he heard the thing come crashing to the ground. He had gone and bagged himself a drone. It had looked like a ball of light with a well-lit dome attached underneath. A modern day drone having a loud speaker and smelly device obviously wasn't tied into the hamlet's downfall, no way. The following day my bud took the contraption to the junkyard and tossed it in a trash can. He wasn't about to give it back to the rightful owner even if he came calling for it. I suspect the jerk was some inventive genus that never grew up and thought it OK to annoy people. When asked why he destroyed such a fabulous flying contraption by shooting it down, Abe had the perfect answer. He was just exercising his second amendment rights."

Story 9

ALERT

You can't trust them, so keep your distance. Some people don't think the scamps exist, that they only survive in folklore. In other words they simply roam the pages of story books and the likes. You'll learn who they are soon enough, so turn the page and get started.

Wee Folk

The stories about to be told are basically fabrications. In other words, I'm lying through my teeth … well maybe not. I'll let you decide. The tales deal with what some refer to as the wee folk, perhaps better known as leprechauns of Irish descent. Rarely seen, they are considered a gathering of big time rascals wherever they reside. These pint sized dudes are supposed to have a pot of gold with them. This seemed unlikely to me since the little hellions didn't appear capable of lifting heavy loads. Besides, I've never witnessed the treasure, neither has anybody else, and I came to suspect the gold thing was pure rubbish. Time's a wasting so on with one of my theoretical projections.

I came to suspect wee folk don't live in Ireland anymore. The reason being, my wife and I visited this island of multiple shades of green for a spell a few years back and never heard them mentioned once – my reason for assuming the leprechauns had departed their homeland. Even more likely, I imagine the rascals became too rowdy and got kicked out. I've come to befriend several such wee ones hereabouts in Montana, the Butte area to be exact, and they all have a story to tell about their daily lives, O'Brien being the first.

"Why do you think the Hatfield's and McCoy's stopped their feuding," he says to me yesterday? "It's like this: I threatened to take up residence in the neighborhood if they didn't!"

"Knowing you as I do, I can believe it."

Soon after, I ran into Casey. "Good day to you, sir, and how are you faring of late? Oh, I see your right hand is badly swollen. What happened?"

"I had a fight with a hobbit earlier."

"A fight with a hobbit? How can that be? Why they're a peace loving people. You must have started the tussle."

"NO, NO, he did."

"How's that?"

"He said 'good morning' to me."

"And you say he started the fight by saying good morning? I don't understand, please explain."

"He wished me a top of the morning before I had my coffee."

"Oh, now I see."

Just a few minutes ago I bumped into O'Leary. "What keeps you busy these days, my man?"

"As you know, I'm the financial advisor of our little community."

"Tell me, do your people really have a pot of gold stashed away?"

"Nooo! Our treasure was too hard to move every time that damn rainbow pointed to it. So … I sold the gold and bought a few high quality gems."

"Diamonds?"

"Yes and I got a fabulous deal."

"So you're a good negotiator?"

"The best."

"And how did you pull off the transaction?"

"I told him I'd beat the crap out of him if he didn't."

Now that my story is concluded, I strongly recommend you don't decide this narrative is a fabrication, or one of my pint sized buddies just might pay you a visit.

Story 10

Beware

Sometimes it's best to leave well enough alone, especially a fenced-in mansion with a shocking history. There are those who don't heed warnings. Beanie is one such person. Read on.

Vacant Stone Mansion

Trouble spreads its tentacles in strange ways, latches onto unsuspecting victims and draws them in. One unfortunate fellow about to be put to the test goes by the name of Beanie. There is no beginning to this tale. It just sort of happens one day for him after years of passing by a fenced in estate on his way home from school. This is no ordinary fencing. It's substantial wrought iron, a ten foot high enclosure topped off with massive, intimidating spearheads. The barrier cloaks a couple of country miles and encompasses a three story stone mansion with an ominous history – disappearances, unsolved murders. Designed to keep out wannabe intruders, the extensive bulwark seems to work ... or does it?

The entranceway, comprised of a rectangular stone structure, supports a heavy iron gate ... a padlocked heavy iron gate. This medieval looking magnificence dominates Elm Avenue but terminates the street. Before the abbreviated street gives way to a gate, bungalows randomly line the old cobblestone roadbed, five on each side. Strangely enough, not one faces the other and none were constructed side by side. Trees grow between homes and provide unplanned, unwanted privacy. Beanie lives a stone's throw from the estate. His girlfriend, Martha, resides across the street cattycorner to his house.

For years rumors circulated around town. The last occupant had been brutally murdered several decades earlier. Townie rumor mills insist his killer resides inside the mansion. After several local inhabitants heard shrieking one evening, two law officers went to investigate. One was stabbed to death. His murder remains unsolved to this day. The surviving officer believed the murderer lived there. All of this occurred before Beanie was conceived.

Nearby residents recently swear they've seen lights filtering through woods within mansion boundaries and, at the same time, heard some-one screeching. It is easy to see why people never bought those remaining lots on Elm Ave and built homes. Many have come to believe evil mortals or possibly tortured souls have taken over the manor, roam the estate and would foil anyone reckless enough to confront them.

There's a knock on the door. A pleasant young lady, who goes by the name of Martha, responds in a most amiable manner – a bubbly demeanor accentuated by her bobbing blonde ponytail. "Yes," she says, opening the door. "Oh, it's you, Beanie," she squeals, "come on in."

"I just finished a late supper, and have to move on before it gets any darker. On the way home from school, I noticed the mansion gate's padlock was missing."

"Don't tell me you're going to investigate the place."

"Exactly! Want to come along?"

"Wish I could, but I can't. I have tons of homework, two nights worth actually. If you must do this investigating thing of yours, I don't want you to go alone. Hold off and I can make it in a couple of days. Do we have a deal?"

"Of course we do, Buttercup," he says, as she looks longingly into his freckled face.

Beanie reaches out, squeezes her hand gently and leaves. She puts on a sad face, then smiles and waves goodbye with her fingertips.

The sun is about to set. Darkness seems to be in a hurry to take command of the landscape, but fragments of light still squeeze between tree trunks barely illuminating neighborhood properties. Beanie has little time to look around. He promised Martha he wouldn't do any investigating. Rationalizing, Beanie decides looking around isn't quite the same as investigating, so he hurries off toward his latest objective. The massive gate is ajar. As he remembers, it had been closed earlier. Taking a deep breath he glances between two bars. Nothing unusual is visible. It appears like always, a bit darker than most places. A thick canapé of leaves overhead blocks most light. Some places even have moss growing between and on the cobblestones. He notices, for the first time, it is a path not a continuation of their street. Well, maybe he was wrong about the gate not being open earlier when considering he was wrong about the path.

Gingerly pushing on the heavy gate, he barely squeezes through and begins his walk. A secluded cobblestone path, lined with evenly spaced maple trees, seems like nature's way of guiding him to his destination, although the mansion is nowhere to be seen. He has never laid eyes on the great house. Obviously, his objective has to be in this direction, if common sense prevails. Continuing on, overhead trees take on a new appearance. Sinister dead branches reach out in all directions creating a spider web look. Darkness creeps in. Is this how a careless fly might recognize an ensnarement … too late? Another unpleasant thought crosses his mind – the disappearances. An unlocked gate lured him into fenced-in mansion grounds much like the hapless fly enters a spacious spider's web. Whoever opened the gate could lock him inside. Is this how it goes down? The thought adds to Beanie's apprehension. Regardless, he trudges on.

The path veers right and into an open area. A three story stone mansion looms before him, cast in the gloom of approaching night. Suddenly a flash of lightening immediately followed by a loud clap of thunder causes him to jump back.

"Yikes!" he yells.

It was more than Mother Nature's display that made him leap. A man's hideous, angry face appeared in a third story window … he thinks. It happened so quickly Beanie can't be certain. He begins rationalizing. Storm clouds illuminated by lightening could take on many shapes, including gruesome faces, and reflect off windows.

While he mulls over this disturbing incident, several rapid flashes of lightening rake the sky and light up mansion windows once again. Mesmerized, Beanie never looks toward the third floor window. Instead, he focuses on an open front door. Shocked and bewildered, he takes off running faster than he ever ran before.

Passing under dead limbs and then through overhead deciduous trees, he prays the gate isn't closed and locked. Before reaching the entranceway, a dark form captures his attention. A beast seems to be keeping pace with him. The ebony creature glides effortlessly around and through dense entanglements of bushes and saplings with little exertion.

"I must be imagining it." He retreated to his feel-good security blanket, rationalizing.

Finally, he reaches the gate. His heart sinks. The gate is closed. "Damn!" With great effort, he pushes and pulls hard on its sturdy, cold handle. The massive metal enclosure creaks open, and he squeezes through. "Phew, I'm out!"

Looking back, there is no visible shadowy creature. "I was scared stiff and my imagination must have been in overdrive."

The next day passes quickly, and Beanie finds himself standing before the gate exactly as he remembers leaving it last night, partially open. Recalling his anxieties, he begins to wallow in deep pools of uncertainty. "Was a dark creature keeping pace with me?"

Once inside, the shackles of doubt are cast aside. Jogging and reminiscing do the trick. Today he learned the owner lives in England, doesn't visit, plans on retiring in a few years and spending summers here. No one has access to the mansion or grounds according to his sources. Soon, the stone mansion stands before him in ever darkening shades. The door isn't visible at first glance. Moving closer he sees it's closed.

"Well, maybe the wind blew the thing shut last night," he reasons.

The door can't be opened. It must be locked. This makes Beanie uncomfortable, quite jumpy. Unwanted bonds of uncertainty return. Determined to move on, he begins to circle the mansion and inspect each window for the hideous face he'd seen, or was it a mere reflection. Windowsills are twelve feet above ground level, making it impossible to see much of the rooms. The back entryway is locked. Hurrying along, Beanie starts to believe nothing is out of the ordinary. His source could be misinformed. Perhaps a guard is employed to perform periodic inspections. That could account for locked doors and unlocked front gate. This emerging feel-good sensation soon comes to an end. The same third story window with a face showing the previous night now has a lit table lamp.

First Beanie breaks into a jog then runs as fast as his feet can carry him. Once again he feels overwhelmed until he's on the other side of the closed gate, then the rationalizing starts as usual.

"It's very likely that same person who checked out the mansion put a timer on a lamp. He would set it to turn on as night approaches. I should have thought things through before bailing out."

Beanie could be right, then again –

Well after supper the next day, Beanie and Martha sit on her front porch. Beanie feels obliged to bring her up to date regarding his findings. She doesn't take too kindly to his just looking around when promising not to investigate. Nevertheless, he is forgiven. She's always forgives him.

Martha isn't so sure the trek in is a good idea. When Beanie suggests they have nothing to worry about and will leave if she becomes a tiny bit uncomfortable, she feels somewhat relieved, and the expedition is a go.

"I made it in and out twice and lived to tell about it." This wasn't very reassuring.

"You see, like I said, we have nothing to worry about. Let's not forget that we're both good runners if bad guys confront us." Whoops, he did it again.

"You were in escape mode twice, running for your life, Beanie Mac Cliff." By his facial down-in-the-mouth expressions, she understands that he really wants to make the trek. "OK, I said I'll go. Now don't start rationalizing if I show concern, and please stop telling me we have nothing to worry about," Martha says, wondering if she made the right decision.

"You got my word on that, Cupcake," he says, all smiles.

Walking on a cobblestone path with Martha, in the light of day, reminds him of a stroll in the park unlike his first two jaunts at dusk. The sun won't set for another full hour. This gives them plenty of time to investigate. Martha wants to leave before night settles in.

It doesn't take long before they approach Beanie's objective. The mansion appears menacing as ever in the shadows of approaching night.

Martha is the first to speak. "Look at the windows ... no curtains. I've never seen such an eerie looking place. It's evident that no one lives here."

They walk up the dozen or so front steps together, holding hands.

"The last time I was here someone had locked the door."

"Think we should knock?"

"Nooo," he says, pushing down on the latch. It was still locked. "Darn it!" While he tries again, Martha shades her eyes and peers into a window.

"Beanie, all the furniture is covered with white sheets. This is common practice when people leave a place for long periods of time."

As they contemplate their next move, Martha broaches a subject that should have been considered before their trek. "You know, Beanie, what we're doing might be construed as trespassing, and if we enter the mansion we could be arrested for breaking in."

"OK, you've got a point. I'll knock, and if nobody answers, let's head back."

"Spoken like a wise man, Beanie Mac Cliff. Actually, I will feel much better if you knock."

He lifts the heavy iron door knocker and lets it bang against its metal plate. Seconds pass and Beanie repeats the procedure. BANG! BANG! No one answers.

Looking uncomfortable, Martha wants to leave. As they start to descend the steps, a loud metal clanking noise alarms them. They're about to run when the door springs open a crack and two tiny black kittens waddle out. Cautiously, Martha and Beanie sit on the top step waiting for them to arrive. Could this be a trap?

A half hour of playing, petting and scratching comes to an end. It is time to head for home as the sun plummets into the western mountains.

"I can't remember ever enjoying myself more. Those two kitties are adorable," Martha says, as she stands to leave.

"Agreed," Beanie bellows, obviously liking the unexpected encounter but still a little leery.

A soft meowing draws the little ones to the door then a pleasant purring lures them inside.

"Come my darlings, have your milk. And you, good friends, may visit my babies any time and … eventually me."

Beanie doesn't say anything to Martha on the way home, but can't help wondering who or what was behind the door. Rationalizing once again, he decides there must be a housekeeper inside with cats.

Who was actually doing the talking? Was it really a housekeeper? If I were Beanie, I wouldn't try to find out!

Story 11

Preface

Political party ideologies continue to go in separate directions. One wants to destroy the other and take complete control of our country, perhaps totally disregarding citizen interests. How do these battles for domination progress as technologies improve? Read more and see one person's views of the future.

Ziggy Twinkledust & Venus

It's the weekend, and Ziggy Twinkledust, better known as ZT for obvious reasons or just plain Ziggy, is kinda hanging out. This model citizen, who appears to be a normal human being in his sector, doesn't have a job. There's no need for one. He's considered a typical progressive in the 25th Century. Some call ZT a robot. That would explain his political tastes perfectly in this so called advanced forward thinking administration. We find him relaxing in a 20 by 20 foot module watching a hologram.

The 25th Century mirrors the early 21st in some respects, especially in political thinking. There are advancements as you might expect. Houses are obsolete – actually not wanted – in this subdivision. Satisfy your needs by thinking up whatever you want, plug your request into a handheld processor and presto, it materializes. Cars aren't necessary. Mentally tell the processor where you want to go and you're instantly there. All this is paid for by automatically deducting the cost from overdrawn bank accounts. It's called deficit spending. This idea became very popular in the 21st Century. Just print more money and kick the can down the road. Unfortunately, they're reaching a point where the sector can't afford a can to kick or equipment to print the money.

This particular day has ZT awaiting his best friend and boss, Venus. She is one of the few who has a single name in their assigned federation. She likes ZT a lot, preferring less complicated men, if you can call them men. The woman, if you can call her a woman just because she uses public bathrooms marked for women, brings bad news to Ziggy.

Across town, we find life advancing at a much slower pace. These life forms are referred to as humans, actually conservatives. Human numbers have been dwindling ever since a string of radical liberals were elected president. Even so, they live in houses, are married, have families and go to church on Sundays if they choose. Liberals keep trying to mandate these ridiculous practices out of existence with some success by treating conservatives as the enemy.

It would appear in the near future that the more tolerant humans will be completely replaced, wiped out, by progressive practices. These relentless robotic types are forced to think alike by their self-serving leaders. Uppity socialists call themselves the New World Order of Manufactured Life Forms. They don't appear to have souls and believe they're better equipped to take over, to rule and to do everything. As a group they do get things done. This accelerated advancement comes by stuffing their minds full of mush like political correctness. Unable to agree on anything, it's harder and takes longer for conservative humans to develop. If they are to stop the trend, tending toward extinction, they must come together, kick out their do nothing leaders and take drastic measures.

Venus is now inside ZT's cubical giving him the bad news. "I'm sorry Ziggy, but you must be terminated. Your time is up. You have to make way for the new and improved models. It's our way of life. We're obligated."

"But Venus, I would like to live longer, if it's alright with you of course. I'm not worn out and have many good years ahead of me. Besides, I'm a transgender robotic human."

"First of all, Ziggy, you are not human. As a progressive you can't be. You don't sleep, eat grown and raised food or have a heart. As your superior, do as I say. Call everyone in your unit and instruct them to open their chests, reach in and crush their obsolete computers. Then, crush yours – got that?"

"Yes, Venus, as you wish my love."

Now finished with ZT, the woman proceeds to the next complex while eating a p b and j sandwich as she goes. Eating a sandwich? Wait a sec. She must be a human masquerading as Venus. All is not lost. It seems mankind is about to make a comeback. Rapid advancements in the world of computer robotics moved the New World Order of Heartless Manufactured Life Forms forward but became their Achilles heel in the doing. Not to worry progressive robots, human conservatives will screw up. They always do. And, they can't ever get anything done, can't pull the trigger so to speak. Whoops, I shouldn't use that expression. It's not politically correct.

Story 12

Beware

How would you feel if you were hunted by dogs and men in Jeeps? A young couple is destined to experience the challenge. And … what exactly are the men's objectives? Decide for yourself.

 Hunted

There are incidents some folks would label criminal while others might regard them as imaginations running wild. One such case that comes to mind is a hunting scheme, hunting human beings for sport – how appalling. For starters, I never caught the beginning of this strange saga or learned of the reasons behind it. But if you bear with me, I'll lay the narrative before you as the prey lived it, and let you pass judgment.

Two people a couple of years beyond their teens but still full of pizazz are found hustling down a small woodsy trail in the middle of nowhere. One, the young redheaded fellow, goes by the name of Antsy. He can't stay still for two seconds together. The other, a young lady, is called Bling, likely because of her sparkling eyes and bubbly smile.

They stop briefly to catch their breath. Antsy glances at his watch. He seems to be rather nonchalant under the circumstances. "We have another thirty minutes before they let the dogs loose and the men, all ten of them, come looking for us or the other couple, in their jeeps."

"Yes, Antsy, and how can we possibly avoid being shot? I certainly didn't like the looks of those characters back there. They positively will overtake us in no time." She kinda seems to regret taking up this unusual challenge at the request of her boyfriend. The scrunched up expression on her face tells all.

"Just follow me, we'll be OK. I sort of know the area some. I've seen it on a map. And take a glance at those acres and acres of awesome Ironwood trees growing close together over there?"

"Well, yes, I see them. I also see the deep ravine to our right. It's so steep it scares me to look down."

"The trees are exactly what I've been looking for," he says. "It's perfect terrain for us. Hunters' jeeps will never penetrate them. Those babies will slow down their progress big time. They'll have to come after us on foot."

"Great, Antsy, let's go for it!" And they do, weaving their way through stands of thin but sturdy trees.

Bling presumes that Antsy has a plan besides just slowing down the hunters. "You have anything else in mind for heading this way?" she says, while sidestepping Mother Nature's obstacles.

"Yes. I don't exactly know where we are, but my gut feeling tells me we're angling toward a decent size river … if I'm right. And if I'm not, we will surely be shot with a barrage of paintballs!"

"Does getting hit with paintballs hurt much, Antsy?"

"Nah, not too much."

Bling doesn't ask any more questions after his response. Perhaps she doesn't want to know, or maybe she's too winded to ask. For whatever reason, they continue on in an easterly direction. Antsy is obviously a woodsman. He's using the sun to guide them.

Coming to a sudden halt, he cups his ear with one hand and places a finger vertically to his lips with the other, his way of asking for silence. A look of mild concern takes over his face. "I hear jeeps coming down the path we were on!"

"I can't rush around anymore, Antsy. I'm, bushed. Give me a few minutes to recover."

"OK. See those rocks up ahead, Bling?"

"Yes, of course."

"When we get to 'em, leave the trail we're now on. Jump on that big flat rock to the right and stay put until I come back. OK?"

"Gotcha!"

She does as told while Antsy continues on for a good hundred feet or more, stops and begins to slowly walk backwards keeping his feet in the slight indentations he had made. Finally reaching the flat rock, he rejoins Bling. She looks baffled until he explains. "I'm trying to confuse the dogs. A hound won't likely pick up our scent on rocks and will continue along the tracks I just laid down over there."

She gives him a head nod, a weary smile and follows him.

Antsy moves south now, not in the easterly direction he eventually intends to go. He plans on staying the course until running out of rocks to step on. The rocky trail soon peters out, ending alongside a knee deep stream. Scent trails don't exist in water.

"Perfect," Antsy says. "Follow me and don't be so glum." Not looking forward to a struggle in cold water, he feels the same way but doesn't tell her as they wade into ice chilling water. In minutes their lower legs and feet go numb.

The sound of jeeps is no longer heard, but an occasional baying hound is, and it's a lot closer than expected. Those hunters are apparently much faster than the two of them. Will the dog become confused at the rocks, the stream? Only time will tell.

The clear stream is a bit strenuous going but negotiable by stepping over smaller obstacles or wading around bigger rocks.

A half hour later, shivering uncontrollably, the pair reach a hundred foot wide, slow flowing river where the stream they traversed dumps its icy water.

"Perfect," Antsy says, "exactly what I'd hoped to find. This water is still cold but a little bit warmer, so let's thaw out by swimming to the other side. We must keep to the shallows as long as possible and head south." Both were encouraged by not hearing a howling dog at the time.

"I suspect this means their pooch lost our scent trail," Antsy says, shaking like a leaf.

Still feeling cold, the two drowned rats drag their frozen carcasses from the river, climb the bank and continue on. They couldn't take any more frigid water.

"I really, REALLY didn't care for the way the one guy glared at us, Antsy. His staring frightened me. He looked creepy, a genuine nutter."

"Nah, you're making something out of … what in the hell was that?"

"What did you hear, Antsy? TELL ME."

"Can't be sure, but I think I might have heard two rifle shots in the distance. We better get out of here in a hurry," he says, spurred on by the sound. "I can only hope the other couple is alright. I don't have one good reason to think this so-called paintball hunt is legit."

"Right you are, Antsy. There could be a sinister side to this trek we're on. I feel it in my unsettled stomach. We can't treat this as a game any longer, OK?"

"You got it right, Bling. I have the same gnawing in my gut."

Time passes. Warming up, they pick up the pace even more. It was Bling who heard the sniffing. She nearly screamed but realized the dire consequences of any unintended reactions. Instead she put her hand over Antsy's mouth and whispered into his ear. "A dog is right behind us!" Instinctively, they slip into the river and frantically swim for the other side. As they burst out of the water the dog howls. This brings three hunters to the river's edge where the young people had just crossed.

Antsy and Bling can't see them but are able to hear the men talk, as they squat behind thick undergrowth, shivering from their swim.

"You sure they entered the river here, Rex?" one man says to the dog.

"This better not be another one of your blunders, daug. I'm dang tired of 'em. I think your sniffer is broken," growls a second man.

"Stop the crap," a third man chips in. "We know they crossed this ice bucket of a river again, so let Rex try some sniffing around on the other side. Maybe he'll do a better job of picking up the trail over there."

Antsy beckons for Bling to move on, and the two take off quickly. When beyond hearing distance they begin conversing at rapid fire speed.

"Did you hear that, Bling?"

"Yes I did, but how could that third hunter possibly know we crossed the river? I suppose it's conceivable the dog's actions led him to the conclusion."

"I don't believe any of them had faith in the dog."

"Right you are, Antsy. Think the third guy heard us swimming?"

"NO! We must have tracking devices on us, that's how. They gave us drinking water, so, I suspect the devices were stashed in our canteens. That explains how they found us so quickly. Oh yes, and they utilize the dog to cover up their use of tracking devices."

"Let's toss them right now," she says, starting to yank the over-sized flask off her belt. "I can do without the water."

"Don't! I have a better idea. Remember the overlook to the right of the Ironwood trees?"

"Yes, how can I forget that hellish chasm?"

"We're going to race up the hill we came from, gulp down a big swig of water and toss our empty canteens into the ravine, then, take off along the trail." And they do. Antsy is convinced the hunters will follow the tracking devices into the ravine.

Later, Bling has second thoughts. "If those three eventually believe the dog, Antsy, we will be in big trouble."

"And if they don't, we will be home free, unless other hunters pick up our trail."

Just before dark the two come upon a cabin. Antsy knocks on the front door while Bling peeks into a window and screams.

Corpses lie on their backs in pools of blood with their eyes and mouths wide open. "How horrible, Antsy. Two people were killed … shot in the chest I think!"

Before he can join her, the pair hears a jeep coming down the road. Both bolt for the woods. Standing behind trees they follow the vehicle with their eyes, hoping it doesn't stop. A hound would surely pick up their scent. Sitting on the backseat, a floppy eared mutt enjoys sticking his head out of the window and letting air blow his ears straight out. Mercifully, the jeep continues on.

"Whew, that was a close call," Bling says, still upset. "You heard two shots fired, and I found two people murdered. Just think, we were seconds away from being shot ourselves."

"Probably! Did you notice the elaborate top end of the jeep's antenna? It was pointed toward the ravine side of the trail. I'll bet our tracking devices are floating downstream in the canteens, and that bunch is searching for us in the gorge."

"You're right on. It's a good thing you suspected the canteens had tracking devices hidden in them. In my opinion, it's the only way to account for the hunter's actions."

"Let's head for the river at the crack of dawn," he says, "and follow it south until we get outta here, while the hunters look for us along the ravine. In the meantime, we'll walk a while before bedding down in the woods for the night."

"We should be perfectly safe now, Antsy." And they were.

The next afternoon we find them sitting in a sheriff's office telling him their story. By his looks, the sheriff doesn't seem to take the couple seriously.

"I'm totally aware of paintball doings in the vast north woods area. Those law breakers don't have a permit for their activities, but they aren't murderers. If they had caught up with you, you would've been paintballed."

"But ... but, what about the poor dead people I saw," Bling says.

"They were likely dummies set up to scare you, same with the two shots you heard, Antsy. This is how those warped minded folks get their kicks. They pull dirty tricks on folks. Did you see them with guns?"

"No."

"Now be off with you, I'm a busy man."

The sheriff could have considered the young couple's take on the trek highly questionable in view of their continuous speculating and lack of hard evidence. Although ... Bling did believe she saw two dead bodies in the cabin.

Obviously, the man with a badge seemed to have a mind set against them from the beginning. Think it had anything to do with his having a dog at home by the name of Rex?

F. Tumbeity Bio
& Other Goodies

Unforgettable highlights in my life impacted the medley of *WOW* short stories. NASA's Moon Lander mission is but one of the pinnacles.

For starters, I served my country during the Korean War. After fighting ceased, my unit shipped to Japan where a legendary thug roamed streets in the darkest nights. *The Phantom of Sasebo* mystery covers my exploits.

College was the next step. The head of the English Department heaped praise on my fertile imagination and urged me to become a writer. Instead, I opted for a degree in math.

Once again in the real world, I helped NASA with their death defying space craft projects. Remember when the Moon Lander's takeoff back to earth was temporarily botched? The rocket engine refused to start. I had inspected and given my approval to the switch that wouldn't turn on. Imagine how I felt at the time. Fortunately, it wasn't a faulty part. The rocket engine didn't fire up due to an easily fixed loose wire. Problem solved and the astronauts returned home safely- PHEW!

The Moon Lander project made me think about space travel and a slog into the future, as a writer of course. These ideas resulted in two tongue-incheek sci-fi short stories, *The Beginning and Ziggy Twinkledust & Venus*.

Moving on, I worked as a plant statistician and designed experiments to pinpoint problems for befuddled engineers. The conundrums were mostly caused by complex process interactions and were typically unpredictable, much like the bulk of my short story endings. I got the idea from the experiments. *Murder Knocks Twice* and *The Peanut Butter*

Sandwich Caper are two prime examples and not what you would expect to find in narrative wrap-ups.

Bottom line: This *WOW* medley of twelve stories is not only based on highlights from the past and extrapolations into the future but also fictitious musings in the present. Look hard and you'll spot a few daubs of dry humor as well. By the way, that Phantom of Sasebo guy scared the crap out of me.

Frank Tumbelty

Look for these books coming soon
by Frank Tumbelty and his charming wife
Lynn!

Deadly Inheritance

The Keeper

Now You See It

The three are a trilogy of mystery adventures.

www.ingramcontent.com/pod-product-compliance
Lightning Source LLC
Chambersburg PA
CBHW060133260626
47160CB00005B/2096